Great-Grandfather, the Baby and Me

Story and Pictures by Howard Knotts

Atheneum 1978 New York

LIBRARY OF CONGRESS CATALOGING IN PUBLICATION DATA

Knotts, Howard.
Great-grandfather, the baby, and me.
SUMMARY: His great-grandfather's reminiscence about
traveling for miles across the sparsely
settled prairie to see a new baby helps a young boy
come to grips with his own
apprehensions about meeting
his baby sister.
[1. Babies—Fiction.   2. Brothers and sisters—
Fiction.   3. Grandfathers—Fiction]   I. Title.
PZ7.K7615Gr   [E]   78-2940
ISBN 0-689-30656-3

Published simultaneously in Canada by
McClelland & Stewart, Ltd.
Manufactured in the United States of America by
The Book Press, Brattleboro, Vermont
First Edition

FOR ILSE

Well, I'm driving into town this morning," Daddy said.

"To see Mommy in the hospital?" I asked.

"To bring your mother home," said Daddy, "and your new baby sister, too."

And off he went with Great-Grandfather and I waving good-bye.

And then I turned and ran down the hill to the creek. I sat down and watched the water running over the rocks and the way the light on the water was always changing, but this time it didn't help. My eyes got wet, and I couldn't keep from crying.

I didn't want to cry, but I just couldn't keep from it. Daddy said he and Mommy were going to call the new baby Mary Alice, but I didn't know who she was. They could just as well have called her Muriel or something. I didn't know who she was.

And then I didn't want to be alone anymore, and I went to look for Great-Grandfather. I found him where I knew he would be, under the apple tree reading. If the morning was nice that was where he always went with his paper or a book.

He could see I was trying to stop crying when I sat down next to him, but he didn't say anything. He just put his arm around me, gave me a squeeze and went on reading. I wanted to ask him what he thought about the baby, but somehow I couldn't.

After a while I knew Great-Grandfather was talking, telling one of his stories. But I didn't listen. I just leaned against him and looked up at the little bits of blue sky I could see when the wind moved the leaves. And then I began to feel better. That's the way it is. Great-Grandfather lives with us and is very old, and lots of times being next to him I feel better.

I guess I must have started listening to Great-Grandfather because I stopped seeing the leaves of the apple tree and saw a field of yellow wheat instead. The land was flat and wide, and there were hardly any trees and the sky was very big. It was harvest time a long time ago, and Great-Grandfather worked in the field.

"How old were you?" I asked.

"Sixteen," said Great-Grandfather.

"And where was this?"

"Canada," said Great-Grandfather. "I'd run away from the orphan home when I was thirteen and I traveled around and took any job I could get just to eat. And that was the summer I helped the Canadians harvest their wheat."

"And why did you travel?" I asked. "Why didn't you stay in one place?"

"I was afraid they would catch me and send me back to the orphan home," Great-Grandfather said.

"Where was Great-Grandmother?" I asked.

"Oh, I met her much later," Great-Grandfather said. "She made me my first real home." I had never met Great-Grandmother, but sometimes Great-Grandfather took me with him when he put flowers on her grave.

"Tell about the wheat and the sky," I said.

It had all happened a long, long time ago, but when Great-Grandfather told it, I could see everything. I could see how it was.

The days were long and hot and the work was hard and the sky was very big. You could look all

around and not see a house. The country wasn't
much settled yet, Great-Grandfather said.

After the hot day the night would turn cold, and
Great-Grandfather slept on the ground in a tent.
Sometimes a wild strong wind blew across the land,
and the night got colder still.

Great-Grandfather and the other men got their
meals from the cook's wagon. They ate early in the
morning and again at the end of the day when the

sun was going down. They ate a lot, Great-Grandfather said, because the hard work made them hungry.

"Sometimes it got so hot, so hot," Great-Grand-father said, "and you'd get so terrible thirsty. You had to go for water to little springs here and there in the fields. But the water was always bitter."

"Bitter?" I said.

"Bitter water," said Great-Grandfather. "Al-kaline, they called it."

"And you drank the bitter water?"

"Had to," Great-Grandfather said. "It was all we had. With bitter water you're always thirsty."

Sometimes at night wild stormy rains came, and once Great-Grandfather's tent blew down.

But other nights were clear and still and the sky would be bright with stars.

"So many stars," Great-Grandfather said, "I never saw so many stars. I don't know why, but all those stars made me lonely."

On Sunday the work stopped and the men would rest. "But there was not much to do, you know," Great-Grandfather said. "It was big, wide, empty country. No towns, not many trees, and the few houses were miles apart, and there was all that sky above your head."

One day news came to their camp that a baby had been born in one of those faraway houses. "And

a friend of mine and I," Great-Grandfather said, "de-cided to go see the baby."

"Go see the baby?" I said.

"That's what people did in those days in that part of the country. What you might call homes were a long way apart, and there weren't many babies. So when a new one came along, it was something to go and see. My friend borrowed some horses for us."

When Sunday came, Great-Grandfather got up early. The cook packed them biscuits and bacon for lunch, for the ride to the baby was long. They set out just as the sun was rising over the wheat.

The morning got hot, and a wind started up. "But it didn't cool us," Great-Grandfather said, "just blew dust in our eyes. My we were glad when it stopped." They had to ride for miles and miles.

Finally by early afternoon they came to the house of the baby. It wasn't big, but it had a front porch and it stood in a grove of trees. Other people were already there. They stood on the porch and under the trees and around a well in the yard.

"The shade was wonderful," Great-Grandfather said. "It was good just to stand in the shade."

"And then did you see the baby?" I asked.

"Not right away," Great-Grandfather said. He said the man of the house came over to him and his friend and asked where they were from. They told him, and he said, "You boys must be thirsty. Have a drink at the well. You'll find the water sweet."

"Not bitter?" I asked.

"Sweet water," said Great-Grandfather as if he were tasting it again. "The sweetest, coolest, loveliest water I ever had in my life. And when we finished drinking, he told us to fill our canteens."

"And then did you see the baby?" I asked.

"Yes," said Great-Grandfather, "then we saw the baby." And he told how the woman brought out her baby, and everyone took turns going up on the porch to look.

"And what did the baby do?" I asked.

"Oh, nothing," said Great-Grandfather. "Absolutely nothing. The baby just slept."

"Just slept?" I said.

"The whole time," Great-Grandfather said, and he gave me a squeeze. "Well," he said with a funny smile as if he were still remembering, "well, we didn't go all that way so the baby could look at us. It was the other way around you know. In that big empty country with all that sky you just got so lonesome in your heart you *had* to go see that baby."

"And then what happened?" I asked.

"We thanked the woman," said Great-

Grandfather. "We told her it surely was a fine baby. We thanked the man. We said good-bye. We couldn't stay long, you know, it was such a long ride back."

And Great-Grandfather told how it was riding through the afternoon, watching the sun get lower and lower and finally go all the way down. I could see him and his friend under the sky riding as the stars came out.

Great-Grandfather stopped talking, and we were back under the apple tree. We just sat there quietly, watching a blue jay rustle some leaves. After awhile I said I was thirsty.

"Let's go in the house," said Great-Grandfather.